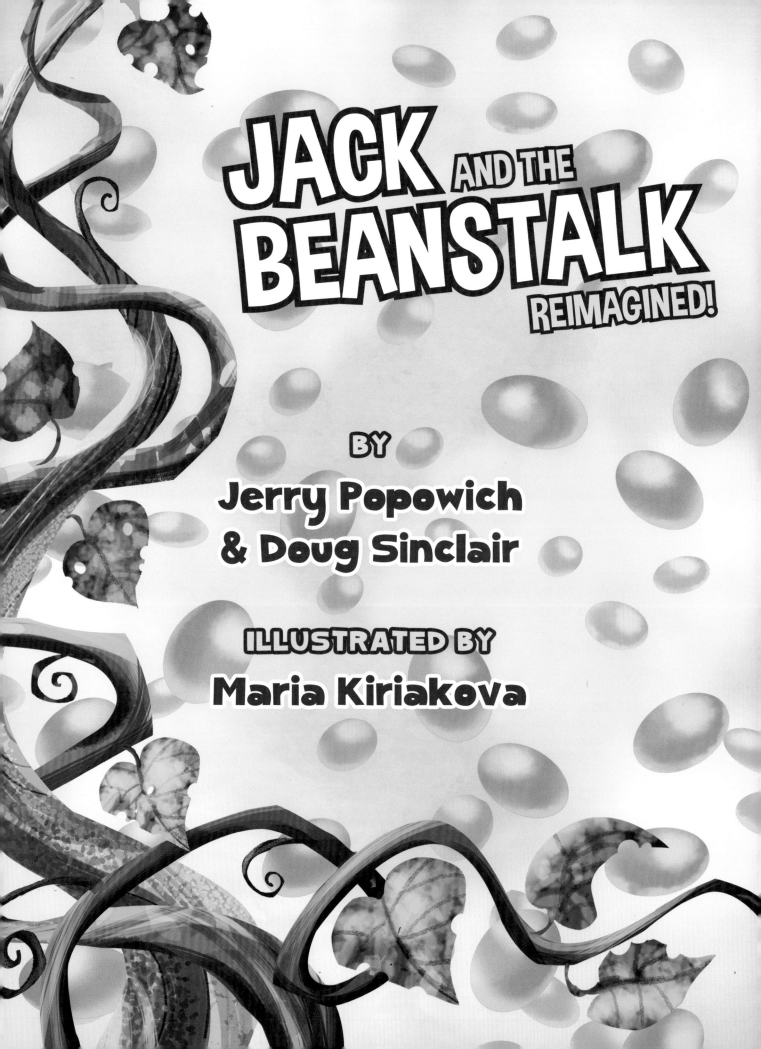

JACK AND THE BEANSTALK REIMAGINED!

BY

Jerry Popowich & Doug Sinclair

ILLUSTRATED BY

Maria Kiriakova

INSTRUCTIONS

1

DOWNLOAD THE FREE MOBILE APP!

Scan the QR code or visit www.incredebooks.com/apps. Look for the Jack and the Beanstalk - Reimagined app and download the app on your iOS or Android device.

2

READ, THEN LOOK FOR SPECIAL PAGES!

Read the book and look for this symbol on special pages. There are four pages that contain special 3D games!

3

WATCH THE PAGES COME TO LIFE IN 3D!

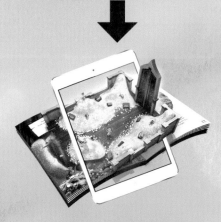

Launch the app and hold your smart phone or tablet facing the book page that contains the symbol. Make sure the entire page is visible. Now watch the page come to life in 3D!

FIND OUT MORE INFORMATION AT WWW.INCREDEBOOKS.COM

Once, there was a boy named Jack.
He and his mother were very poor.
They lived in their tiny, leaky cottage, and they owned one cow.
They didn't even like the cow very much.

One day, Jack' mother said,
"We will have to sell the cow.
Wash your feet and take it to the market,
and be sure to make a good trade."

So, Jack went off to market.
He wasn't sure what a "good trade" meant,
but it seemed like something he'd know when he heard it.

4

Jack was tired from all the walking.
Just as he was about to stop for a rest,
he met a man who didn't look suspicious at all.
"I'll make you a deal," said the man.
"I'll trade your cow for these beans. They might be magic."

7

Jack thought that beans were probably not
"a good trade" for a cow, but beans that might be magic
might be "a good trade."

So, he traded with the man and skipped home with his prize.

When Jack got home, his mother was not happy with his deal.
Angrily, she threw the beans out the window.
Since they were so hungry,
eating the beans would have made more sense,
but that's not what she did.

Jack trudged off to bed.
He was thinking that only a very big surprise
could save them now, but as if that would happen.

That night, while Jack and his mother slept, a surprise grew.
And grew…and grew…until it was a very *big* surprise!

When Jack awoke, he found a beanstalk
growing outside of his house.
It was a beanstalk so big and so tall that
it reached all the way above the clouds.

13

Though still tired from yesterday's walk to the market, climbing as high as the clouds seemed like something he could manage.

So, up the beanstalk he clambered.

14

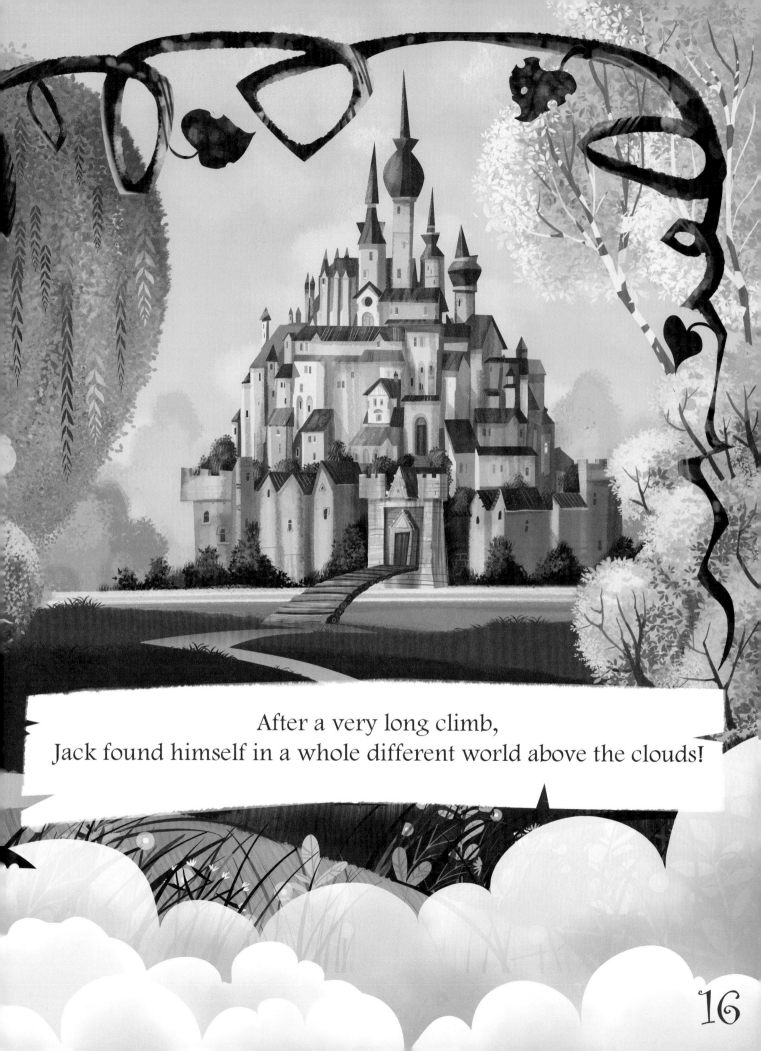

After a very long climb,
Jack found himself in a whole different world above the clouds!

Soon, Jack came upon the biggest castle
he had ever seen.
From the size of the gate, he thought
a Giant must live there.

"I better not knock," thought Jack.
"If the Giant is sleeping, it would be rude to awaken him."
Of course, this is just another way of saying,
"I'm going to sneak in."

18

Jack felt very small as he
crept through the castle.
He saw wondrous treasures,
the likes of which he could have never
possibly imagined.

Can you imagine a harp that magically plays itself?
Or a goose that lays golden eggs?
Well, these are the wonders that Jack saw.

Suddenly, the floor began to tremble
from giant footsteps: BOOM! BOOM! BOOM!
Then, a horrible voice thundered:
"Fe, fi, fo, fum, I smell…I smell…"

"…feet! That's what I smell. I smell feet!"
Jack scolded himself for not washing his feet.
Sometimes, his mother was right.

The Giant scooped Jack up in his giant hand and roared with fury, "What are you doing sneaking around in my…in my…"

But before he could finish, the Giant yawned so big and so wide that Jack could have tickled his tonsils.

Honk! Honk! Honk! Honk! Honk!

"What's the matter, Giant?" Jack asked.
"Are you tired?"

"It's that blasted goose," replied the Giant.
"All night with the honking, honking, honking!
I can't even hear my harp playing a lullaby
to put me to sleep."

24

Just like that, Jack had an idea.
"Giant," he asked, "what if I take the goose home with me?
Then you could have all the rest that you need.
Would that be a good trade?"

27

And Jack and his mother lived happily ever after.

The End